A Conscience Is...

by Max and Hylma Armstrong

illustrated by Barbara Pride

STANDARD PUBLISHING
Cincinnati, Ohio   3602

Library of Congress Cataloging-in-Publication Data

Armstrong, Max.
  A conscience is—.

  Summary: Discusses our gift of conscience which
lets us know right from wrong.
  1. Conscience—Religious aspects—Christianity—
Juvenile literature. [1. Conscience. 2. Conduct of
life] I. Armstrong, Hylma. II. Pride, Barbara, ill.
III. Title.
BJ1278.C66A75 1986   241'.1   86-3806
ISBN 0-87403-122-2

A Conscience Is...

Have you ever wondered, *What is a conscience? Does everybody have one? Where did your conscience come from?*

There is a little warning *voice* that goes off like an alarm clock inside you! It's called your conscience. You probably remember it going off, warning you, and giving you advice like, "Do this!" or "Don't do that!"

Your conscience is one of the most amazing gifts you have. It is something you were born with . . . like the ability to breathe, think, and move. It tells you right from wrong.

How do you suppose your conscience got so smart? It listens a lot to what you say and think. It also listens to what your parents, teachers, and friends tell you.

Your conscience is your secret, private, and special gift from God—like your own personal Ten Commandments!

One of the most common things your conscience tells you is "Don't cheat!"—in school or any place. You may want to copy or look at somebody else's answers during a school test. Those answers do *not* belong to you!

If you don't cheat, you can always look at
yourself in the mirror in the morning and say,
"I may not always make the highest grades in
school, but at least they are *my* grades! I *never*
cheat! My conscience won't let me!"
Congratulations!

You can also say, "I don't steal, either! My conscience won't let me."

Congratulations ... again!

The temptation to steal happens often.

Your mother, daddy, brother, sister, or even a friend may carelessly leave some money or something else of value lying around.

You know how easy it is to think *Take it, nobody will ever know who did it.*

... But you and your conscience will know! And that little warning voice inside you remembers for a long time.

Have you ever said these words?
"Hey, Mother, I'll do it later!"
... it happens all the time.
You get busy, and mother interrupts you by saying,
"Please take out the trash ... sweep up the leaves ... or wash the dishes, NOW!"
But you are busy working on some really important project. You can't be expected to just quit what you are doing
... or can you?

Down deep inside, you and your conscience
know that somebody has to do these jobs. If
you don't, then Mother will. And you sure
don't want to add more work to what Mother
does.

About that time your conscience comes to the
rescue and urges you to be fair and do the job
now. Then you both feel a lot better.

Now there are some real serious things to think about with your conscience. What about smoking, drugs, drinking, and cussing?

Here is a little verse that is important to remember.

> Roses are red and violets are blue,
> God's divine spirit is a part of you!

Remember God put you here and gave you the power and strength to move all the many parts of your body. You need to ask yourself this question.

"Would I want to dump garbage like alcohol, drugs, smoke, and bad words on God?"

Remember God loves you and does not want you to put anything in your body that will hurt you and keep your body from being healthy.

Ask your conscience, then listen to what it tells you.

Sometimes you have to make the decision
whether to help or hurt?

You have a chance to pay back that mean kid
down the street

... really get even with him

... really hurt the meany.

But you don't! Do you know why? Suddenly
you and your conscience remember some wise
words mother and daddy said to you. They
said, "God put you here on earth to *HELP*
others, not to hurt them."

... Remember?

Sometimes it is difficult to be honest. It is easy to just tell part of the truth, or to add to the truth to keep yourself from getting into trouble with mother, daddy, and especially friends.

The only trouble with this is that you and your conscience know that those silly actions are dishonest.

Lots of smart boys and girls like you learn that it is better to always mean what you say. So be careful about saying things you don't really mean.

Do you fib or tell lies?

Your conscience never lets you forget what you said. So remember to tell the truth. Be honest with yourself and others.

Now, this is very personal stuff ... but it happens all the time, so you should be prepared.

You, and only you, own your body! Plus God, of course, because He gave it to you.

Sometimes some of your friends, even a stranger, or maybe a close relative may try to touch or rub the private parts of your body.

That's when you should immediately talk it over with your conscience. It is sure to tell you this truth.

"Never let *anybody* touch or rub your private parts, regardless of *whom* it is. It is not only improper, but it is *WRONG!* Report it immediately to an adult you can trust!"

By the way, a private part is any part of your body that is covered by your swimsuit.

Have you ever wondered why you have two ears but only one mouth?

The answer is so you can listen more and talk less.

God sure knew what He was doing when He put the human body together, didn't He? God knows that anybody learns more by listening than talking. Even your conscience listens to what you say and think.

Sometimes when you feel lonely or maybe even disappointed, here's some good advice ... talk to your conscience.

People won't think you are nuts, and you will be surprised how much that little warning voice can help.

Next to God, mother, and daddy, you can always trust your conscience.

Your conscience is like listening to the Ten Commandments, and you can't go wrong obeying them!

Are you one to blame others for something you did? Other kids sure don't like anybody who always says, "I didn't do it! He did it."

It is easy to point the finger, but that is not the way to make friends
... with your conscience or others.

You will always end up hating yourself for blaming others for something *you* did.

Think about this. A very smart person once said to a very lonely person:

A man that has friends must be friendly.

Remember to make friends you first have to be a friend.

Ask yourself, "Who are the best liked kids in school?"

The friendly boys and girls are, of course. Because they seem to think of you first and themselves second.

Remember, everybody is looking for a friend ... a real friend! Let your conscience help you be a friend.

Here's a good motto of life for you to follow.

Never do anything to anybody you would not like for that person to do to you.

It is also called being fair, like putting yourself in the other person's shoes.

If somebody ever asks you, "Who is the *most* important person in the world?" how would you answer?

According to one of those TV Quiz shows, many youngsters gave this answer, secretly, of course, "I Am!"

... but they are not, and neither are YOU! You are important, but God is *most* important!

If it wasn't for God, you wouldn't even be here. Also you wouldn't have a conscience to give you advice or help you make the right choices!